# Judy Moody
## Declares Independence!

Megan McDonald is the award-winning author
of the Judy Moody series. She says that most
of Judy's stories "grew out of anecdotes about
growing up with my four sisters". She confesses,
"I am Judy Moody. Same-same! In my family
of sisters, we're famous for exaggeration. Judy
Moody is me … exaggerated." Megan McDonald
lives with her husband in northern California.

You can find out more about Megan McDonald
and her books at **www.meganmcdonald.net**

Peter H. Reynolds says he felt an immediate
connection to Judy Moody because "having
a daughter, I have witnessed first-hand the
adventures of a very independent-minded girl".
Peter H. Reynolds lives in Massachusetts, just
down the road from his twin brother.

You can find out more about Peter H. Reynolds
and his art at **www.fablevision.com**

**Books by Megan McDonald
and Peter H. Reynolds**

*Judy Moody*
*Judy Moody Gets Famous!*
*Judy Moody Saves the World!*
*Judy Moody Predicts the Future*
*Judy Moody: The Doctor Is In!*
*Judy Moody Declares Independence!*
*Judy Moody: Around the World in 8½ Days*
*Judy Moody Goes to College*
*Judy Moody, Girl Detective*
*Judy Moody and the NOT Bummer Summer*
*Judy Moody and the Bad Luck Charm*
*Stink: The Incredible Shrinking Kid*
*Stink and the Incredible Super-Galactic Jawbreaker*
*Stink and the World's Worst Super-Stinky Sneakers*
*Stink and the Great Guinea Pig Express*
*Stink: Solar System Superhero*
*Stink and the Ultimate Thumb-Wrestling Smackdown*
*Stink and the Midnight Zombie Walk*
*Stink and the Freaky Frog Freakout*
*Stink-O-Pedia: Super Stink-y Stuff from A to Zzzzz*
*Stink-O-Pedia 2: More Stink-y Stuff from A to Z*
*Judy Moody & Stink: The Holly Joliday*
*Judy Moody & Stink: The Mad, Mad, Mad,
Mad Treasure Hunt*

**Books by Megan McDonald**

*The Sisters Club*
*The Sisters Club: Rule of Three*
*The Sisters Club: Cloudy with a Chance of Boys*

**Books by Peter H. Reynolds**

*The Dot • Ish • So Few of Me*
*Rose's Garden • Sky Colour*

# Judy Moody
## Declares Independence!

HUZZAH!

Megan McDonald

illustrated by
Peter H. Reynolds

WALKER
BOOKS

This is a work of fiction. Names, characters, places and incidents
are either the product of the author's imagination or, if real,
are used fictitiously. All statements, activities, stunts, descriptions,
information and material of any other kind contained herein
are included for entertainment purposes only and should not be
relied on for accuracy or replicated as they may result in injury.

First published 2005 by Walker Books Ltd
87 Vauxhall Walk, London SE11 5HJ

This edition published 2011

26

Text © 2005 Megan McDonald
Illustrations © 2005 Peter H. Reynolds
Judy Moody font © 2003 Peter H. Reynolds

The right of Megan McDonald and Peter H. Reynolds to be identified as
author and illustrator respectively of this work has been asserted by them
in accordance with the Copyright, Designs and Patents Act 1988

Judy Moody ™. Judy Moody is a registered trademark
of Candlewick Press Inc., Somerville MA

This book has been typeset in Stone Informal

Printed and bound in Great Britain by Clays Ltd, St Ives plc

All rights reserved. No part of this book may be reproduced,
transmitted or stored in an information retrieval system in any form
or by any means, graphic, electronic or mechanical, including
photocopying, taping and recording, without prior written
permission from the publisher.

British Library Cataloguing in Publication Data:
a catalogue record for this book
is available from the British Library

ISBN 978-1-4063-3587-3

www.walker.co.uk

In Memory of Jon and Mary Louise McDonald
M. M.


To Diana GaiKazova, who declared independence
and is making history of her own
P. H. R.

# Table of Contents

Judy Moody

Judy Moodington

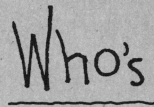
Who's

Dad

Richard John-Hancock Moody

Mum

Kate Betsy-Ross Moody

John Hancock

Fancy First Signer
of the Declaration of
Independence

Tori

Not a Tory; fab collector
of sugar packets

# Who

## Sybil Ludington

Sybil La-Dee-Da,
Girl Paul Revere

## Paul Revere

Bellringer,
false teeth maker,
midnight rider

## Stink

Town crier, fond
of musical toilets

## Frank

## Rocky

←————→

Partners in Crime:
The Boston Tub Party

# Bean Town, MOO-sa-chu-setts

HEAR YE! HEAR YE!

She, Judy Moody, was in Boston! Bean Town! As in Mas-sa-chu-setts. As in the Cradle of Liberty, Birthplace of Ben Famous Franklin and Paul Revere. Land of the Boston Tea Party and the Declaration of Independence.

"Boston rules," said Judy.

Three best things about Boston so far
were:

> 1. *Freedom from two whole days of school*
>    *(including one spelling test, two nights of*
>    *homework and a three-page book report)*
> 2. *Freedom from riding in the car next to Stink*
>    *for ten million hours*
> 3. *Freedom from brushing hair every day*

She, Judy Moody, Rider of the First Subway in America, was finally on her way
to the real-and-actual Freedom Trail! The
place where her country started. Where it
all began.

The American Revolution! The Declaration of Independence! Freedom!

R A R E!

Judy and her family climbed up the stairs and out into the fresh air, heading for the information booth on Boston Common, where Dad bought a guide to the Freedom Trail.

"Did you know there used to be cows right here in this park?" asked Stink. "It says so on that sign."

"Welcome to MOO-sa-chu-setts!" announced Judy. She cracked herself up. If Rocky or Frank Pearl were here, they'd crack up too.

"Just think," Judy told Stink. "Right now, this very minute, while I am about to follow in the footsteps of freedom, Mr Todd is probably giving Class 3T a spelling test

back in Virginia. Nineteen number-two pencil erasers are being chewed right this very second."

"You're lucky. I had to miss Backwards Shirt Day today."

"The trail starts right here at Boston Common," Dad said.

"Can we go and look at ducks?" asked Stink. "Or frogs? On the map there's a frog pond."

"Stink, we're going on the *Freedom* Trail. Not the *Frog* Trail."

"What should we do first?" asked Mum.

"Tea Party! Boston Tea Party Ship!" said Judy, jumping up and down.

"We came all the way to Boston for a *tea party*?" asked Stink.

"Not that kind of tea party," Mum said.

"The people here first came over from England," said Dad, "because they wanted to have freedom from the king telling them what to do."

"Dad, is this another LBS? Long Boring Story?" asked Stink.

"It's way NOT boring, Stink," said Judy. "It's the beginning of our whole country. This wouldn't even be America if it weren't for this giant tea party they had. See, the Americans wouldn't drink tea from over there in England. No way."

"Not just tea," said Mum. "The British made them pay unfair taxes on lots of things, like stamps and sugar. They called it the Stamp Act and the Sugar Act. But the Americans didn't have any say about what all the tax money would be used for."

"I don't get it," said Stink.

"We didn't want some grumpy old king to be boss of us," said Judy.

"America wanted to be grown-up and independent," said Mum. "Free from England. Free to make up its own rules and laws."

"So Thomas Jefferson wrote the Declaration of Independence," said Dad.

"And a lot of important people signed it real fancy," said Judy, "like John Hancock, First Signer of the Declaration. Right, Mum?"

"Right," said Mum.

"Before we hit the Freedom Trail, let's go

and see the Liberty Tree," said Dad. "That's where people stood to make important speeches about freedom."

"Like a town crier?" asked Judy.

"That's right," said Dad. "Here we are."

"I don't see any tree," said Stink. "All I see is some old sign on some old building."

"The British cut it down," Dad said. "But that didn't stop the Americans. They just called it the Liberty Stump and kept right on making speeches."

"I don't see any tree stump," said Stink.

"Hello! Use your imagination, Stink," said Judy.

"Kids, stand together in front of the sign so Dad can take your picture."

"I still don't see what's so big about the American Revolution," mumbled Stink.

"Some of us like the American Revolution, Stink," said Judy. "Let freedom ring!" she shouted. Hair flew across her face.

"Judy, I thought I asked you to use a brush this morning," Mum said.

"I did use it," said Judy. "On that pink fuzzy pillow in our hotel room!" Mum poked at Judy's hair, trying to smooth out the bumps. Judy squeezed her eyes shut, making an Ouch Face. Dad snapped the picture.

"Hear ye! Hear ye!" called Judy. "I, Judy Moody, hereby declare freedom from brushing my hair!"

"Then I declare it from brushing my teeth!" said Stink.

"P.U.," said Judy, squinching up her nose.

Dad snapped another picture.

Three worst things about Boston so far were:

    *1. Stink*

    *2. Stink*

    *3. Stink*

# The Freedom (from Stink) Trail

"Time to hit the Freedom Trail!" said Dad.

"Let's head up Park Street," Mum said, pointing to a line of red bricks in the pavement. "Follow the red brick road!"

"Look!" Judy cried, running up the hill. "Look at that big fancy gold dome!"

"That's the State House," said Mum, "where the governor works."

"Judy!" Dad called. "No running ahead. Stick close to us."

"Aw," said Judy. "No fair. This is supposed to be the *Freedom* Trail."

"Stay where Dad and I can keep an eye on you," said Mum.

"Roar!" said Judy.

❧   ❧   ❧

After the State House, Mum and Dad led them to Park Street Church, where the song "My Country 'Tis of Thee" was sung for the very first time.

Stink looked for famous-people initials carved into a tree outside. PLOP! Something hit Stink on the head. "YEE-UCK! Bird poo!" said Stink. Judy cracked up. Mum wiped it off with a tissue.

Stink sang: *"My country pooed on me*
*Right near the Pigeon Tree.*
*Of thee I sing..."*

"Mum! Dad!" said Judy, covering her ears. "Make him stop!"

Judy ran ahead. "Hurry up, you guys! The church has an old graveyard!"

Mum stopped to read the plaque on the gate at the entrance: "'May the youth of today ... be inspired with the patriotism of Paul Revere.'"

"Paul Revere's grave is here!" Judy shouted. "So is John Hancock's, First Signer of the Declaration. For real!"

Judy saw gravestones with angel wings, skulls and bones, and a giant hand with one finger pointing to the sky.

"'Here lies buried Samuel Adams, Signer of the Declaration of Independence,'" Dad read. "Did you know he also gave the secret signal at the Boston Tea Party?"

"'Here lyes y body of Mary Goose,'" Stink read. "Boy, they sure did spell funny."

"And I thought I was the world's worst speller," said Judy. She took out pencil and paper from her backpack and made a rubbing of Mother Goose's grave. Stink made a rubbing of a skull and bones, a leaf and a crack in the pavement.

"Do we have to keep seeing stuff?" Stink asked when they got to the Ben Franklin statue. "So far it's just a bunch of dead guys and some old stuff that isn't even there any more."

"But what about the Boston Tea Party?" asked Judy.

"AW!" Stink whined. "I have to go to the toilet."

"Stink, don't be the town crier," said Judy. "I mean, the town *crybaby*!"

"Tell you what," said Mum. "Dad, why don't you and Judy go and see the Paul Revere House? I'll take Stink to the toilet, and we'll meet back here."

"Great idea!" said Dad.

 toy    toy    toy

Judy and Dad walked and walked. At last they came to 19 North Square. "Did you know that Paul Revere made false teeth?" Dad asked. "And he made the first bells in America. He even drew cartoons."

"Wow!" said Judy. "All that on top of riding his horse lightning-fast and warning everybody that the British were coming!"

"That's right," Dad said. "A friend of Paul Revere's climbed out of a window and over a rooftop to give the lantern signal from the Old North Church: one if by land, two if by sea…"

"Star-spangled bananas!" said Judy.

"And it says here he rode all the way to Philadelphia to tell them the news about the Boston Tea Party," Dad said.

"Tea party? Did somebody say *tea party*?" asked Judy.

"OK, OK. Let's head back to meet Mum and Stink."

Judy ran up to Stink. "You missed it, Stink!" She told him all about the guy climbing out of the window and giving the secret signal.

"Who cares?" said Stink. "We saw something better!"

"What?" said Judy. "A two-hundred-year-old toilet?"

"No, a *musical* toilet!" said Stink. "You put a coin in—"

"You have to pay to go to the toilet?" Judy asked. "That stinks."

"You go inside, and you're in this round room, and it's all white and clean – really, really clean – and it plays music!"

"I thought he'd never come out," Mum said.

"C'mon. We can quick hop the subway over to the Tea Party Ship," said Dad.

"Finally!" said Judy.

"More old stuff? I declare NO FAIR!" Stink shouted.

# Sugar and Spies

She, Judy Moody, declared independence from Stink. She ran up the planks ahead of him. She climbed aboard the *Beaver*, the Boston Tea Party Ship!

"Is this a real ship?" Stink asked.

"It's a real ship," said a guy wearing a wig and dressed like Paul Revere. "But it's not old, like the real *Beaver*. We built it to show what the Tea Party ship looked like."

"Finally! Something NOT old!" said Stink.

Judy climbed some ropes. So did Stink. She tried out a hammock. So did Stink. She went down the ladder into the dark cargo hold. So did Stink.

"Stink! How can I declare independence from you if you keep following me everywhere?"

Judy went back on deck. The Wig Guy was explaining about the men who wore disguises, sneaked aboard ship after dark and threw a million dollars worth of tea overboard.

"Who'd like to try throwing tea into Boston Harbour?"

Judy rushed to the front. Stink followed (of course!). They picked up bales tied with rope. Judy heaved a bale of tea over the side. "I won't drink tea! Taxes are NO FAIR!"

"Take that, King George!" said Stink as he tossed a bale off the ship.

"Who else wants to try?" Wig Guy pointed to a girl wearing bunny ears and carrying a bag that said BONJOUR BUNNY.

"C'mon, now. Wouldn't you like to give 'er the old heave-ho?"

"No," said the girl. "I quite like tea." She had a funny accent.

"From England, are you?" asked the man. The girl nodded.

"How exciting. This lass has come all the way from *across the pond,* as they say, just to see our ship!" The girl beamed.

"Glad to have you aboard, lassie!" Wig Guy shook her hand. "The Revolution was a long time ago. Let's be mates!"

The girl with the freckles and the funny voice was from England! Where they drank tea and had a queen. Judy had never met a real-live person from a whole other country before. Rare!

"I'm going to talk to her," Judy told Stink.

"You can't! She's a Redcoat! One of the Bad Guys!"

Judy looked around, but the Girl from

Across the Pond was nowhere in sight. Just then, Mum called for Judy and Stink to go to the gift shop.

Judy wandered up and down the aisles. Boxes of tea, bags of tea, tins of tea. Teapots and teacups and teaspoons. Stink followed her.

"Look! A tricorn hat!" She tried it on. "Stink, can I borrow some money? I want to get this hat."

"It's my money," said Stink. "From my allowance. Use your own."

"But I already spent mine at the Old North Church gift shop. On a Declaration of Independence and a *Paul Revere's Ride* flip book. I should get more allowance because I'm older than you. C'mon, Stink. You always have money."

"No way," said Stink.

"Redcoat!" Judy said.

"Yankee Doodle!" Stink said.

"Lobsterback!" said Judy.

"Chowder Head!" said Stink.

"Red Belly!" said Judy.

"Blue Belly!" said Stink.

"Kids! Keep it down," said Dad.

"Stink, stop following me around and stop getting me in trouble. Don't forget, I'm independent of you now." Judy walked away, past the drums and pennywhistles.

There she was! The tea drinker girl from England was not even looking at tea.

She was looking at snow globes. Of Boston. Judy liked snow globes too!

"Are you really a Red – I mean, from England?"

"Of course," said the girl. Her voice sounded snooty, as if the queen herself made the girl's bed.

"Does the queen make your bed?" asked Judy.

"WHAT?"

"Never mind. I was just wondering. What's your name?" Judy asked.

"Victoria. But you can call me Tori."

Stink popped up from behind a spinner rack. "Tory! Tories were the Bad Guys in the Revolution!" he said.

"Stink, stop spying on us!" said Judy.

She turned back to Tori. "Um ... what's that rabbit on your bag?" she blurted.

"It's Bonjour Bunny. I'm freaky for Bonjour Bunny! I have the backpack, jimjams and sleeping bag. I even have my own Bonjour Bunny alarm clock! I just got the phone for my birthday. And the flannel, I mean washcloth, for my bathroom in our flat."

"Flat? You have a tyre in your house?"

"No, it's our apartment. Mum has her bathroom and I have mine."

PHONE! BATHROOM! WASHCLOTH! Judy's mum and dad would never let her have a phone. Or her own bathroom. At home, Judy had to use any old washcloth. Even ones with Stink cooties.

"I collect stuff too," said Judy. "Mostly Barbie-doll heads and pizza tables. My newest collection is ABC gum. I stick it on the lamp in my room."

"ABC gum?" asked the girl.

"Already Been Chewed – I label each piece, like a rock collection."

"Fab!" said Tori. "I've never heard of that."

"And I collect pencils," said Judy. "And Band-Aids."

"Brilliant!" said Tori. "We call them plasters, not Band-Aids."

"Do you collect tea?" asked Judy.

"No. But I do collect sugar packets with pictures on them." Tori opened her purse. It was filled with sugar packets! She, Judy Moody, Collector of the World, had never even *thought* of collecting sugar packets.

"I have American presidents and flags of the world," said Tori. "Famous paintings. Hotel names ... boring! Famous women, too. See? Here's one of Susan B. Anthony."

"Do you have Amelia Bloomer? She gave a speech on Boston Common in her undies," said Judy.

"In her knickers?" asked Tori.

"Really they were bloomers. Some people call them pant-a-loons. Because they're *loons* if they think girls can't wear pants," said Judy.

"At least it wasn't in her nuddy pants,"

Tori whispered. "That means *bare naked*!"
Judy and Tori cracked up.

"I did get some at the cafe with Ben
Franklin sayings!" Tori added. "See?"

Judy read the
sugar packets.
"'Don't cry over
spilled milk.'
'If your head is
made of wax,
don't stand out
in the sun.'" She

cracked up some more. "Brilliant!" said
Judy. "My little brother will be so jealous!"
She looked around. She didn't see Stink
anywhere.

"The short one? Been spying on us? Maybe he's gone to the loo."

"The what?" Judy asked.

"You know." Tori pointed to the toilet.

"The loo! That's cuckoo!" Judy didn't see her mum and dad either. "Well, I'd better go and find my family," she said. "We're supposed to eat lunch at the snack bar."

"Me too! I'll go and fetch my mum."

"See you there," said Judy.

"Cheers!" said Tori. "Wait – what's your name?"

"Judy. Judy Moody."

"Brilliant!" said Tori.

# In a Nark

Judy found Mum, Dad and Stink at the checkout. Dad was getting a ship-in-a-bottle kit to make a model of the *Beaver*. Mum was buying stuff to sew a cross-stitch pillow of the Paul Revere statue with the Old North Church in the background. Stink was holding a tin of Boston Harbour tea and waving a flag with a snake on it that said, DON'T TREAD ON ME.

Judy paid for her hat (with Stink's money), and they walked to the snack bar.

"You owe me four dollars and ninety-seven cents plus tax," said Stink.

"Tax! Mum! Dad! Stink's going all British on me. I need a raise in my allowance so I can pay him back."

"We'll talk about more allowance when we get home," said Mum.

"Time for lunch," said Dad. "I need a coffee."

"Not tea?" asked Mum.

"Just being loyal to my country," Dad said.

"Can I try coffee?" asked Judy. "I want to be loyal to my country too."

"Dream on," said Dad.

"How about tea?"

"How about chocolate milk?" said Dad.

"The Boston Chocolate Milk Party. How UN-Revolutionary."

Judy ordered a Ben Franklin (cheese toastie with French fries). In the middle of bite three of her Ben Franklin, she said, "Hey, there's Tori!"

"Tori the Tory," said Stink.

Tori and her mum came over. While everybody met, Tori showed Judy all the new Bonjour Bunny stuff in her bag.

"You have all the luck!" said Judy. "I need more allowance. For sure and absolute positive."

"Mum gives me two pounds a week," said Tori.

"Star-spangled bananas!" said Judy. Tori got *pounds* of allowance! All Judy got was a few stinky ounces.

"C'mon," said Tori. "Let's collect more Ben Franklin sugar packets." While the grown-ups talked and Stink blew bubbles in his un-Revolutionary chocolate milk, Judy and Tori sat at an empty table and spread out all the sugar packets.

*A penny saved is a penny earned.*
*Don't cry over spilled milk.*
*Fish and visitors stink after three days.*

"Let's make up our own!" said Judy. She wrote on the backs of the packets:

A penny saved is never as much as Stink has.
Fish and little brothers stink after three days.

"Crikey! That's jolly good!" said Tori. She made one up too:

Don't cry over spilled chocolate milk.

Judy taught Tori how to play Concentration with sugar packets. Tori showed Judy how to build a sugar-packet castle. When it was time to go, Judy did not want to leave her new friend.

"Mum? Dad? Can Tori come back to the hotel with us?" Judy asked.

"Or can Judy go swimming at our hotel with us?" Tori asked her mum.

"Can Tori come to Chinatown with us tonight?"

"Can Judy sleep over at our hotel? We

can sleep on the floor like we do in our flat at home."

Mum looked at Dad. Dad looked at Mum. "I don't think so, honey."

"AW! Why not?" asked Judy.

"We've only just met Tori," said Mum.

"Yes, that's right, girls," said Tori's mum.

"Please, Mum," said Tori. "Judy's so much fun."

"Judy and her family have got their own plans," said Tori's mum. "And we have tickets for the Duck Tour later this afternoon."

"Besides, we have to get an early start in the morning, Judy. It's back home to Virginia tomorrow," Dad said.

"Please-please-pretty-please with sugar packets on top?" Judy begged. "This is our one and only chance. We might never see each other again ever. Please? It would be brilliant!"

Mum shook her head no.

"Not even on account of the Revolution? I'm American and she's British and it's really good if we're friends. We could change history!"

"We said no, honey," Dad said.

"Well," said Tori's mum, "it's been lovely meeting you and your family, Judy. Hasn't it, Tori?"

"Crumb cakes!" said Tori. She hung her head. She kicked at a stone.

"Now, don't get in a nark," said Tori's mum.

"Who's going in an ark?" asked Stink.

"A nark," said Tori's mum. "It means a bad mood."

"Ohh. My sister has narks ALL the time," said Stink.

"Maybe when Tori gets back to London and we get home," said Mum, "you two can write to each other. Like pen pals!"

"That would be lovely," said Tori's mum. "Wouldn't it, Tori?" Tori didn't answer. "Well, we'd better be going," said her mother.

"Here, you can have these," Tori told Judy. "To remember me by." She gave Judy her Bonjour Bunny ears.

Judy gave Tori a whole packet of gum. "You can start your own ABC collection," said Judy.

Tori wrote down her address in London. Judy gave Tori her address in Virginia. "We can send each other sugar packets!" Tori whispered. "It'll be the bee's knees!"

Judy did not feel like the bee's knees.

She, Judy Moody, was in a nark. Not a good nark. A bad nark.

# The Purse of Happiness

Judy was in a nark for four hundred and forty-four miles. She was in a nark all the way through Rhode Island, Connecticut, New York and Pennsylvania. (She slept through Maryland.) She was even in a nark through Home of the Presidents, Washington, DC.

Judy Moody was in a nark for seven hours and nineteen minutes. A Give-Me-Liberty nark.

"Mum! Judy won't play car games with me."

Stink wanted to count cows. Stink wanted to play the number plate game. Stink wanted to play Junior Scrabble.

"Judy," said Mum. "Play Scrabble with your brother."

"It's *baby* Scrabble!" said Judy. "I know. Let's play the silent game. Where you see how long you can go without talking."

"Hardee-har-har," said Stink.

"I win!" said Judy.

"Hey, you two," said Mum.

"It's her fault," said Stink.

"Judy, you're not still in a mood about Tori, are you?" asked Mum.

"You never let me do stuff," said Judy. "You should hear all the stuff Tori gets to do in England! She has tons of sleepovers. She even has her own phone. And her own bathroom! And she gets pounds of allowance. You think I'm still a baby or something."

"Or something," said Stink.

"Judy, if you want us to treat you like you're more grown-up, and if you want a raise in your allowance, then you'll have to show us that you can be more responsible."

"And not always get in a mood about everything," said Dad.

"I've never even had a sleepover before!" said Judy.

"Maybe when we get home, you can have a sleepover with Jessica Finch," said Mum.

"When cows read," said Judy. She, Judy Moody, was moving to England. She chewed two pieces of ABC gum, loud as a cow. She blew bubbles. *Pop! Pop! Pop-pop-pop!*

"She's still in a mood!" announced Stink.

In her mood journal, Judy made up nicknames for Stink all the rest of the way home.

Stinker            Stink Bug
Stink-o-lator      The Stink Man
Stink-o-rama       Stink McFink
The Stinkster      Stink-a-roni

@    @    @

When Judy got home, she dragged her tote bag upstairs to her room. *Thwump, thwump, thwump.* She dragged her backpack, her blanket, her pillow and her sock monkey. And her stuff from the gift shop. She shut the door and climbed up into her secret hideaway (her top bunk).

She, Judy Moody, was supposed to be writing her book report, as in not waiting till the very, very last minute. Instead, she declared freedom from homework.

Then she, Judy Moody, had an idea. A freedom idea. A John Hancock idea. A Declaration of Independence idea.

She did not even stop to call Rocky and tell him about the Boston Tea Party Ship and the Giant Milk Bottle that sold star-spangled bananas. She did not even stop to call Frank and tell him about Mother Goose's grave and the musical toilet.

That could wait till tomorrow.

But some things could not wait.

Judy gazed in awe at the copy of the Declaration of Independence she'd got in Boston. It was on old-timey brown paper with burned edges that looked like tea had been spilled on it. Judy squinted to try to read the fancy-schmancy handwriting.

When in the bones of human events ... blah, blah, blah ... we hold these truths ... more blah, blah ... alien rights ... Life, Liberty and the Purse of Happiness.

She, Judy Moody, would hereby, this day, make the Judy Moody Declaration of

Independence. With alien rights and her own Purse of Happiness and everything.

Judy pulled out the paper place mat she had saved from the Milk Street Cafe. The back was brown from chocolate-milk spills. Perfect! At last, Judy Moody knew what Ben Franklin meant when he said *Don't cry over spilled milk.*

The real Declaration of Independence had been written with a quill pen. Luckily, she, Judy Moody, just happened to have a genuine-and-for-real quill pen from the gift shop.

Look out, world! Judy mixed some water into the black powder that came with the pen, dipped the feather pen into the ink and wrote:

# Judy Moody's
# Declaration of Independence
## (WITH 7 ALIEN RIGHTS)

I, Judy Moody, hereby declare...

- Freedom from brushing my hair
- Freedom from little brothers (as in STINK)
- Freedom from baby bedtime (stay up later than Stink)
- Freedom from homework
- Freedom to have sleepovers
- Freedom to have my own bathroom (and washcloth!)
- Freedom to get pounds of allowance

*Judy Moody*

She signed it in joined-up writing with fancy squiggles, just like Mr Revolution Himself, First Signer of the Declaration, John Hancock. And she made it big so Dad could see it without his reading glasses, just like they did for King George.

Judy ran downstairs wearing her tricorn hat. Where was Mouse? Judy found her curled up in the dirty-laundry pile. She jingled her cat like a bell. "Hear ye! Hear ye!" she called. Mum, Dad and Stink came into the family room.

"I will now hereby read my very own Judy Moody Declaration of Independence, made hereby on this day, the fourth of Judy. I hereby stand up for these alien rights – stuff like Life, Liberty and definitely the Purse of Happiness." Judy cleared her throat. "Did I say *hereby*?"

"Only ten hundred times," said Stink.

Judy read the list aloud, just like a town crier (not town crybaby). At the end, she took off her tricorn hat and said, "Give me liberty or give me death!"

"Very funny," said Dad.

"Very clever," said Mum.

"No way do you get to stay up later than me," said Stink.

"So you agree?" Judy asked Mum and Dad. "I should get all these freedoms? And a load more allowance?"

"We didn't say that," said Dad.

"We'll think it over, honey," said Mum.

"Think it over?" said Judy. Thinking it over was worse than maybe. Thinking it over meant only one thing – N-O.

Then Dad started talking like a sugar packet. "Freedom doesn't come without a price, you know," he told Judy.

"Dad's right," said Mum. "If you want more freedom, you're going to have to earn it – show us you can be more responsible."

Judy looked over her list. "Can I at least have Alien Right Number One? If I didn't have to brush my hair every day, I'd have more time to be responsible."

"Nice try," said Dad.

Parents! Mum and Dad were just like

King George, making up Bad Laws all the time.

"You guys always tell me it's good to stand up for stuff. Speak up for yourself and everything." Judy held up her Declaration. "That's what I just did. But I'm not even one teeny bit more free. That really stinks on ice!"

"Tell you what." Mum looked over the list. "You can have your own washcloth." Dad started to laugh but turned it into a cough.

"Tori has her own phone AND her own bathroom. And pounds of allowance. She can buy all the Bonjour Bunny stuff she wants, without even asking. And she drinks tea. And wakes herself up with her own alarm clock. And she has sleepovers in her flat that's not a tyre."

"We're not talking about Tori," said Mum. "We're talking about you."

Crumb cakes! She, Judy Moody, did not have any new freedoms at all. Not one single alien right from her list. All she had was a lousy washcloth.

"ROAR!" said Judy.

"If you don't want the washcloth, I'll take it," said Stink.

# Huzzah!

Judy went to bed her same old un-free self. But the next morning, she decided Mum and Dad and the world would see a brand-new Judy Moody. A free and independent Judy. A more responsible Judy. Even on a school day.

Judy started by getting out of bed (without an alarm clock) before her mum had to shake her awake.

Next, she brushed her teeth without

complaining. Mum had set out a new blue washcloth – a plain old boring blue wash-cloth, but it was just for her. Judy wrote *Bonjour Bunny* on it, and made the capital *B*s into funny bunny ears.

Then Judy did something she had not done for three days. She brushed her hair (and put on her Bonjour Bunny headband from Tori). A responsible person did not have bird's-nest hair.

Then Judy did something she had not done for three weeks. She made her bed.

A grown-up, independent person did not have a bed that looked like a garage sale.

☙    ☙    ☙

On the bus, Judy told Rocky about the star-spangled bananas at the Giant Milk Bottle and the Sugar Packet Girl named Tori and about throwing tea off the Tea Party Ship. She could not wait to tell her teacher and her whole class.

"What are you going to tell your class about Boston?" she asked Stink.

"The musical toilet," said Stink. "What else?"

When Judy got to school, she told Mr Todd and the whole class all about Boston. "We went on the Freedom Trail and it was so NOT boring, and it's OK I missed my spelling test because I learned stuff there, too, like about Mr Ben Famous Franklin and Paul Revere and—"

"Judy! Take a breath!" said Mr Todd. "We're glad to have you back."

Judy showed them her *Paul Revere's Ride* flip book and explained all about tea and taxes to the class.

"My mum drinks tea and she's not a traitor," said Rocky.

"I went to Boston once to visit my grandpa," said Jessica Finch.

"Sounds like you had quite an educational trip, Judy," said Mr Todd. "Thanks for sharing with us. Maybe I'll read your book aloud in our reading circle today.

First, let's take out our maths facts from yesterday."

Judy multiplied 28 x 6, 7, 8, 9 and 10 until she thought her eyes would pop. At last, Mr Todd announced it was reading-circle time.

"Today I'll be reading a poem Judy brought to share with us from her trip to Boston, called *Paul Revere's Ride*. This poem tells a story."

"I saw his house and his real wallpaper and his false teeth and everything!" said Judy.

"This was my favourite poem when I was a boy," Mr Todd continued. "In school, we had to memorize it and recite it by heart.

It's by a man named Henry Wadsworth Longfellow. The poem is about three men and their famous midnight ride during the American Revolution. One of those men was Paul Revere."

Judy raised her hand. "And one was a doctor!" she told the class.

"Shh!" said Jessica Finch.

Mr Todd lowered his voice to a whisper. Class 3T got super quiet.

"'Listen, my children, and you shall hear
Of the midnight ride of Paul Revere...'"

The poem told all about how Paul Revere rode on horseback through the night to warn each farm and town that the British were coming.

Judy raised her hand again. "Mr Todd, Mr Todd! I saw Ye Olde Church where they hung the lanterns! For real! You know how it says, 'One if by land, two if by sea'? Paul Revere said to light one lantern if the British were sneaking in by land, two if they were coming across the water."

"Did that guy really ride his horse and do all that stuff?" asked Jessica Finch. "Because I never even heard about it the whole time I was in Boston."

"It's true," said Mr Todd. "Paul Revere warned two very important people, Sam Adams and John Hancock, to flee. But before he could warn everybody, he was stopped by the British and his horse was taken."

"But the doctor escaped and warned everybody!" said Judy.

"That's right," said Mr Todd. "You know, there's also a girl who had a famous ride just like Paul Revere. Her name was Sybil Ludington."

Star-spangled bananas! A Girl Paul Revere! Judy Moody could not believe her Bonjour Bunny ears.

"They don't often tell about her in the history books," said Mr Todd, "but we have a book about her in our classroom library."

"Huzzah!" said Judy Moody.

"Huh?" asked Frank.

"It's Revolutionary for YIPPEE!" Judy said.

# The UN-Freedom Trail

She, Judy Moody, was the luckiest kid in Class 3T. Mr Todd let her take the Girl Paul Revere book home. Judy read it to Rocky on the bus. She read it to Mouse the cat. She read it to Jaws the Venus flytrap.

Sybil Ludington lived in New York, and her dad needed someone to ride a horse through the dark, scary forest to warn everybody that the British were burning down a nearby town. Sybil was brave and told her dad she could do it. She stayed up late past midnight and rode off into the dark all by herself. Sybil Ludington sure was grown-up and responsible. She showed tons of independence.

Judy would be just like Sybil Ludington. Responsible. Independent. All she had to do was prove it to Mum and Dad. There was only one problem.

She, Judy Moodington, did not have a horse.

And she would never in a million years be allowed to stay up past midnight.

Crumb cakes! She'd just have to be responsible right here in her very own house, 117 Croaker Road. Starting N-O-W.

Judy went from room to room all over the upstairs. She picked stuff up, put stuff away, hid stuff in the closet. Downstairs, she picked up one cat-hair fur ball, two giant lint balls, her basketball, Stink's soccer ball and Mouse's jingle ball.

Being responsible sure made a person hungry.

Judy stopped to eat some peanut butter out of the jar with a spoon (not her finger!). She stopped to feed Mouse (not peanut butter) and empty out the litter box (P.U!). She stopped to do some homework (without one single peanut-butter fingerprint!).

Mum and Dad were always bugging her to be nice to Stink, so she went up to his room to be nice. She looked on his desk. She looked under his bed.

"What are you looking for?" asked Stink.

"I'm looking for something nice to say," said Judy. "I like that ant farm poster on your wall."

"You gave it to me," said Stink.

"Well, um … your hair looks good."

"Did you put something in my hair?" Stink shook his head. "Eeww, get it out!"

"Stink! Nothing's in your hair. Not even a spider."

Stink plucked at his hair like a dog with fleas.

"I said *not even*! I was just trying to be nice."

Judy never knew independent people had to be so nice. And so clean. But wouldn't Mum and Dad be surprised when they saw all the stuff she could do on her own? Without anybody telling her she had to. She, Judy Moody, would be Independent-with-a-capital-*I*. Just like Sybil Ludington. For sure and absolute positive.

Judy traced her feet onto red paper. *Snip, snip, snip*! She made a trail of red footprints all through the house. Not a messy, drop-your-stuff-everywhere trail. An independent, show-how-responsible-you-are trail. She even made signs for each stop along the way, just like the real Freedom Trail.

Now all she had to do was find Mum and Dad and Stink.

☙    ☙    ☙

"The trail starts here," said Judy. She pointed to the sign in front of a wilted, half-dead plant: YE OLDE LIBERTY TREE.

"First I'll make a speech at Ye Olde Liberty Tree. Hear ye! Hear ye!" called Judy, jingling Mouse again. "Give me liberty or give me more allowance!" Mum and Dad laughed. Stink snorted.

"Listen, ye olde trail people. I'm Judy. I'll be your tour guide. Follow the red footprints to freedom!" Judy led her family from room to room.

On the dining room table, it said, JUDY MOODY DID HOMEWORK HERE.

"I do my homework there every day," said Stink. Judy gave him ye olde hairy eyeball.

On the kitchen floor, Judy pointed to a sign that said, JUDY MOODY FED MOUSE HERE.

"Isn't that one of your chores already?" asked Dad.

"Yes," said Judy. "But nobody had to remind me to do it."

She pointed to the kitchen table: JUDY MOODY ATE PEANUT BUTTER HERE.

"I don't get it," said Stink.

"I ate it with a spoon, not my fingers, and I didn't eat any in my room or get it on stuff," said Judy.

Judy opened the door to the laundry room: Judy Moody Picked Up Lint Balls Here. She opened the door to the downstairs bathroom: Judy Moody Washed the Soap Here.

"I hate the dope who thought up soap," Stink recited, cracking himself up. "I wish he'd eat it. I repeat it. Eat it."

Stink was not helping on the trail to freedom one bit. "Stink, stop saying stuff," said Judy.

"It's a free country," said Stink.

They followed the red footprints up the stairs to Judy's room. A sign on the bottom bunk said, Judy Moody Made the Bed Here. One on the top bunk said, Private! Don't Look Up Here.

"What are all those lumps up there?" asked Stink.

"Next stop, Stink's room," said the tour guide. His door had a sign taped to it: JUDY MOODY WAS NICE TO STINK HERE.

"Were not!" said Stink.

"Was too!" said Judy.

"Ha!" said Stink. "You told me I had a spider in my hair!"

"Last but not least, the big bathroom!" said Judy. JUDY MOODY PICKED UP THE P.U. TOWELS HERE.

"So what do you think?" Judy asked. "Wasn't I super-duper, Sybil-Ludington responsible?"

"This is great, honey. Everything looks

really good," said Dad. "You're starting to show us that you can be responsible and do things independently."

"It's nice when we don't have to tell you all the time," said Mum.

"So I can have more freedoms now? Like not brushing my hair all the time? And staying up later than Stink?"

"I want freedoms too!" said Stink. "Chocolate milk for breakfast!"

"We're proud of you, Judy," Mum said. "But these are all things we want you to do anyway."

"You already get an allowance for doing these things," said Dad.

Tarnation! Judy was in a nark again. The narkiest.

The Freedom Trail was not free at all. The UN-Freedom Trail.

She, Judy Moody, picked up P.U. towels and washed soap and ate peanut-butter-not-with-her-fingers for nothing.

"It's just plain ye olde not fair!" she cried.

# The Boston Tub Party

When Judy got home from school the next day, there was a mysterious package waiting for her.

"It has queens on it!" said Stink.

"It's from Tori!" Judy tore off the tape. "Sugar packets! For my collection!" There were clipper ships and castles, knights and queens. Even famous London stuff like Big Ben and the World's Largest Ferris Wheel, the London Eye.

"Rare!" said Judy. "Here's one in French. *'Je vois le chat.'* Stink, can you read it?"

Stink squinted at the sugar packet. "I think it says, 'Your head is toast.'"

"Does not!" said Judy. "Give it!" She read the back. "It says, 'I see the cat.'"

Judy found some that Tori had made herself, with funny British sayings like nuddy pants and stuff.

Amazed = gobsmacked
Throw up = pavement pizza
Crazy = barmy, off your trolley

"Can I have the pavement pizza one?" asked Stink.

"You're off your trolley, Stink."

"When was I *on* my trolley?" he asked.

Judy read the Bonjour Bunny postcard.

Bonjour, Judy!
Hope you like the
Sugar packets for
your collection—
all the way from
England! Don't
drink too much tea!
   Cheerio!
YNFFE, Tori xox
(Your New friend From England)

POST

Judy Moody
U.S.A.

"There's a bunch of tea bags here too. Real English tea, like at the Boston Tea Party," Judy said. "Tori's barmy if she thinks I'm even allowed to drink all this tea."

"Only traitors drink tea from England," said Stink.

"I'll be a traitor," said Mum. "I'd love to try some English tea." She selected one in shiny blue foil and headed for the kitchen.

Wait just a Yankee-Doodle minute! Judy had a not-so-barmy, off-your-trolley idea. She was gobsmacked that she hadn't thought of it before.

Since Mum and Dad would not let her have more freedoms, she would rise up and protest. Brilliant!

@    @    @

The next day at school, Judy passed notes to Rocky and Frank:

Special TP CLUB
Meeting
SATURDAY 12:00 NOON, MY HOUSE
BE THERE OR BE PAVEMENT PIZZA!

On Saturday, Rocky and Frank rang the Moodys' doorbell at exactly two minutes past twelve. Judy and Stink both ran for the door. Stink got there first. "It's not a Toad Pee Club meeting!" he blurted. "Judy lied. It's a *Tea Party* Club!"

"No way," said Frank.

"I'm not drinking any old tea with a bunch of dolls," said Rocky.

"Not that kind of tea party," said Judy, dragging them up to the bathroom. "C'mon. It'll be fun. Ben Franklin's honour!"

"I see tea bags," said Frank. "And a teapot."

"This is boring," said Rocky.

"Look! It's the talking teapot!" said

Stink. "From when Judy was little." He pressed a button.

"I'm a little teapot," the teapot sang, "short … like … Stink."

"Did it just say 'short like Stink'?" Frank asked. He cracked up.

"No – it said 'short and stout'," said Stink. "The batteries are running out!"

"Forget about the teapot," said Judy. "This is a *Boston* Tea Party." Judy explained about the real Boston Tea Party. "It's a protest! Right here. In the bathtub!"

"What's a protest?" asked Frank.

"You get to yell about stuff that's not fair," said Judy.

"Then I protest having a tea party," said Rocky.

"And you get to dump tea in the bath-tub," said Stink.

"The Boston *Tub* Party!" said Judy.

"The Wig Guy said everybody dressed up and painted their faces so nobody would know who they were," said Stink.

"Way cool," said Frank.

Stink got a bunch of funny hats from his room. "I call the tricorn hat!" said Rocky.

"I have face paints," said Judy.

Frank painted a not-cracked Liberty Bell on her cheek.

"Did you know they rang the Liberty Bell when they first read the Declaration of Independence?" Judy told Frank.

Stink got a moustache. Rocky got a beard. And Frank got a Frankenstein scar.

Judy filled the tub with hot water. "OK, everybody think about stuff that's not fair. Ready? Now, on the count of three, throw your tea into the tub. One, two … WAIT!"

"What's wrong?" asked Frank.

"It has to be dark. The real Tea Party was after dark." She turned out the big light, and the night-light flickered on.

"We can pretend it's the moon," said Rocky. "At midnight."

"THREE!" called Frank. He took the lid off the pot and dumped the tea into the tub. Rocky and Judy ripped open boxes of tea and tea-bag wrappers.

"Hey, let me!" said Stink. "You guys are hogging."

"Stink, you be on the lookout. Blink the light if you hear Dad coming. One if by stairs, two if by hallway."

Stink stood by the door. "You forgot to hoot and holler and yell not-fair stuff," said Stink.

Everybody started yelling and throwing tea bags into the bathtub.

"No more homework!" said Rocky.

"More allowance!" said Judy.

"More chocolate milk!" said Stink.

"No baby-sitting! No litter patrol!" said Frank.

Stink took off his shoes and socks, hopped right into the tub and started acting like a teapot. He made one arm into a handle and one into a spout.

"I'm a little teapot, short and stout," he sang. "When I get all steamed up, hear me shout, 'Give me chocolate milk or give me death!'" He sprayed water out of his mouth.

"Ooh, you spat on me," said Rocky.

"You're getting us all wet!" cried Frank.

Judy thought she heard footsteps on the stairs. "The British are coming! The British are coming!" she warned.

A voice, a deep voice, a *Dad* voice, said, "Hey, what's all the—"

"Abandon ship! Abandon ship!" Judy cried.

"What in the world is going on up here?" asked Dad, opening the bathroom door. "Sounds like an elephant in the bath-tub." He turned on the lights.

Water dripped from the walls like a rainforest. The floor was flooded with giant brown puddles. Stink drip-drip-dripped like a short and stout wet mop.

The tub water was a brown sea of murky, ucky, yucky tea. Tea bags bobbed up and down on the tiny bathtub waves. The Boston Mud Party.

"Judy?" asked Dad. "Stink?"

Stink pointed to Judy. "It was her idea!"

"We were having a Boston Tea Party," said Judy.

"Judy," said Dad. "Just a few days ago, you were showing off this *clean* bathroom."

"But Dad! It's a protest! For more freedoms."

"A mess this size sure isn't going to get you more allowance ... or your own bathroom."

"Pretend this is Boston Harbour. We were just making history come alive. Like homework."

"Sorry. This harbour's closed. Rocky, Frank, it's time for you boys to go home. Judy, no more friends over for one week. And you'd better get this mess cleaned up before Mum gets home. You too, Stink."

"But I don't even want independence!" said Stink. "Just more chocolate milk."

"The Patriots swept up after they threw tea in the harbour," Dad said.

No friends for one week! This was just
like what the British did to the Americans –
one of those Bad Laws they called the
In-tol-er-able Acts. Dad was closing down
the tub just like the Big Meanies closed
down the harbour after the real Tea Party!

Judy felt like stamping her feet (the Stamp Act). She felt like throwing sugar packets (the Sugar Act). She felt like declaring independence *on the wall* (in permanent marker)!

But just like all the Bad Laws in the world did not stop the Patriots, the Clean-the-Bathroom-Again Law and No-Friends-for-One-Week Law would not stop her. And they would not, could not, put her in a nark. They were just bumps in the road on the Judy Moody March to Freedom.

She, Judy Moody, would live by a Not-Bad Law, the Law of the Sugar Packet: *If at first you don't succeed, try, try again.*

# Sybil La-Dee-Da

When Judy got out of bed on Monday morning, she did not stamp one foot. She did not throw one sugar packet. Instead, she quietly-and-to-herself declared independence from brushing her teeth and taking a shower. She did not want to mess up the bathroom again. EVER.

Her book report from when she was in Boston was due today. A book report was NOT going to put her in a bad mood. Even if she had waited till the last minute. Judy decided right then and there to make this her best-ever book report. That's what a responsible person would do.

She dressed up in her pilgrim costume – the one Grandma Lou had made for Halloween. *Ye olde pilgrimme costoom* had an apron and made Judy look just like a girl from the American Revolution. Judy wore regular-not-loony pants underneath the skirt for bloomers. And she made thirteen curls in her hair – one for each of the thirteen colonies.

"Who are you? Heidi?" Stink asked at breakfast.

"None of your beeswax," said Judy.

"Are you a nurse?"

"N-O!" said Judy.

"Hey, I know. You're Priscilla Some-body! Like a pilgrim?"

"No, I'm Revolutionary. The Girl Paul Revere. For my book report today."

"Oh. So you're that Sybil La-Dee-Da?"

It sure was hard to declare independence from bad moods when Stink was around.

"Bye, Mum. Bye, Dad," Judy called on her way out the door.

"Hey, wait for me!" Stink yelled.

"Sorry! I'm riding my faster-than-lightning bike to the bus stop!" Judy yelled back. And she was off.

❧   ❧   ❧

Right before the end of the school day, it was time for Judy's book report. She asked Frank Pearl to help her. They stood up in front of the class.

"Mr Todd? I have a different kind of book report. It's acted out. Like a play."

"Cool!" said Rocky.

"The book I read is called *Sybil: The Female Paul Revere*," Judy told her class. "It's about the Girl Paul Revere. And this," she said, pointing to Frank, "is the Boy Paul Revere. Frank – I mean Paul – is helping me, Sybil Ludington."

Judy started with a poem: "'Listen, my children, and you shall hear / Of a girl who rode way further than Paul Revere.'"

SYBIL: Hey, Paul Revere? Why are you so famous?

PAUL: Because, Sybil Ludington, I rode my horse all night. I warned everybody the British were coming.

SYBIL: I did too. My horse is named Star. It was dark. I was scared. It rained all night. I was brave. It was muddy.

PAUL: It wasn't muddy when I rode.

SYBIL: Well, la-dee-da.

"No fair! It doesn't say that here!" said Frank.

"I just added it," said Judy. "Keep reading."

PAUL: I'm forty years old and I rode sixteen miles.

SYBIL: I'm only sixteen and I rode almost forty miles.

PAUL: I made it to Lexington to warn Sam
Adams and John Hancock.

SYBIL: Hey, Paul? Weren't you caught by
the British?

PAUL: At first I wasn't. Then I was.

SYBIL: Didn't Mr Todd say they took your
horse?

PAUL: Yes.

SYBIL: Aha! So you got caught and didn't
finish warning everybody. I, Sybil
Ludington, DIDN'T get caught,
and I warned everybody. I yelled,
'Stop the British. Mustard at
Ludingtons!' All the British had
to go back on their ships. Then
everybody came to my house for
hot dogs (with mustard). Even
Mr George Famous Washington.
The end.

"Did Sybil What's-Her-Face really eat hot dogs?" asked Jessica Finch.

"She ate mustard," said Judy. "Ketchup wasn't invented yet."

Mr Todd chuckled. "Actually, the word is *muster*, not *mustard*. When Sybil rode her horse to warn everybody, she called them to muster, which means to get together."

"The other parts were all true," said Judy. "I give this book five *really*s. As in really, really, really, really, really good. It was so good, I stayed inside at break to read it. It was so good, I read it to my cat and my Venus flytrap!"

"Thank you, Judy," said Mr Todd. "Sounds like Sybil Ludington really inspired you."

"Everybody should know about the Girl Paul Revere. Most people have never heard of her, because for some barmy reason they forgot to put girls in history books. I wouldn't even know about her if you hadn't told me."

"Maybe some others will want to read the book now," said Mr Todd.

"Sybil Ludington should be in our social studies book for everybody to read about. Girls should get to be in history books too, you know. Especially girls who did independent stuff, don't you think?"

"Yes, yes, I do," said Mr Todd.

"Girls rule!" all the girls shouted.

"Huzzah!" said Judy.

# The Declaration of UN-Independence

On the bus ride home, Rocky told Judy how much he liked her book report. "When I first saw you looking like a pilgrim, I was sure it would be boring. But it was WAY not boring."

"Thanks," said Judy. "I hope I get a way good grade and it shows my Mum and Dad how grown-up and responsible I am."

"Just think," Rocky said, "how super scary it must have been when Sybil rode through the woods … and it was dark and robbers were all around."

"But she had to stop the British from burning down the whole town of Danbury!"

"Yeah. But if she got caught, the bad guys might think she was a spy!" Rocky said.

Judy and Rocky talked about Sybil all the way home.

When they got off the bus, Judy started walking, then said, "Oops, I almost forgot. I rode my bike to the bus stop today."

"OK. See ya!" called Rocky as he loped off towards his house. Judy unlocked her bike. Behind her, the doors of the bus hissed and closed, and the brakes squeaked as it pulled away from the kerb.

Wait ... something was not right.

Stink?

STINK!

Stink did not get off the bus! Stink had never NOT got off the bus before.

❧    ❧    ❧

Judy could not think. She was sure she'd seen him get ON the bus. Should she yell for help? Race home and get Mum?

"HEY!" yelled Judy. "Mr Bus Driver! HEY!" she shouted. The bus was already driving off down the street.

WWBFD? What would Ben Franklin do? Go to bed early? Save a penny? Judy did not think sugar packet sayings could help her now.

There was only one thing to do. Chase the bus!

Mum would worry if she didn't come right home, but there was no time to go and tell her. Not when her brother was being kidnapped by a runaway bus.

She, Judy Moody, had to get her brother back. No matter how stinky he was, he was still her brother.

Judy hitched up her pilgrim skirt and

hopped on her bike. She pedalled hard. She pedalled fast. She rode like the wind. She rode like Sybil on Star. She chased that bus down the street and around the corner and up the hill and down the hill.

Cars whizzed by. *Whoosh!* Dirt flew in her face. She swerved to miss a big hole in the road. What if she fell off her bike and broke her head?

Judy kept riding. She rang her bell. She yelled, "HEY! Mr Bus! My brother's on there. GIVE! ME! BACK! MY! BROTHER!"

The bus kept going.

A dog barked at her. What if a big meany dog got loose and chased her? What if she got bitten by a wild dog? A wild dog with RABIES?

Judy pedalled faster. Wind flapped her skirt and whipped her thirteen curls every which way. A big green dustcart screamed by, way too close. Judy's wheels wobbled. Her handlebars shook. The truck honked at her, *wooomp*, deep like a foghorn. Her heart pounded.

What if she got run over by a P.U. dustcart?

She rode her bike all the way to Bacon Avenue. Traffic! Cars! Trucks! Red lights!

Then she saw it. The bus! The school bus, bright as a big cheese in the middle of the road. It had crossed the intersection and was heading up the hill on the other side of Third Street.

Mum and Dad would FREAK if she crossed the busy street in the middle of traffic by herself. But they might freak more if she came home late ... without Stink!

WWSLD? What would Sybil Ludington do? Sybil would think for herself. Be independent. Be brave.

Judy hopped off and wheeled her bike to the crossing. She waited for the red man on the sign to change to the green man. "Hurry up!" Judy yelled at the light. "The bus is getting away!"

Finally, the light changed. She looked both ways, took a deep breath and crossed the street safely.

Judy hopped back on her bike and zoomed up the hill. *Puff, puff, puff.*

Judy huffed and puffed until she caught up with the bus. "Stink!" she shouted, cycling on the pavement, right alongside the bus. The bus driver looked over. Judy pointed to the back of the bus. "My brother!"

At last! The bus stopped to let some kids off. The door rattled open. "My little brother … *puff, puff* … is … *puff, puff* … on that bus!" Judy yelled.

Stink was already rushing up to the front of the bus. "I fell asleep!" he told Judy. "And then I woke up and you were gone and I didn't know where I was! I was so scared."

"It's OK," said Judy. "I chased you and I found you and you're safe now." Stink clutched her shirtsleeve and wouldn't let go.

"Thank you," she said to the driver. "Thanks for stopping. C'mon, Stinker. Let's go home."

@ @ @

When Judy and Stink got home – over an hour late – Mum was Mad-with-a-capital-*M*. "I thought I asked you to come straight home after school," Mum said. "You scared me half to death!" She said she was scared and worried sick, but she did not look sick. Just M-A-D.

She did not even give Judy a chance to explain. "Judy, you know better than this. Go to your room. Now!"

"Stink should go to his room too. He's the one who fell asleep and—"

Mum's lips turned into a thin white line. "I don't want to hear it!" said Mum. She pointed upstairs.

Judy slunk up to her room, crawled into bed and got under her baby quilt. She, Judy Moody, Friend of Sybil in History, was in trouble again. Trouble with a capital *T*. Worse than the Boston Tub Party.

Grown-ups! They acted like they wanted you to be all independent, but as soon as you were, they went and changed their minds. Independence. HA! All it did was get her in trouble.

Maybe if Judy just declared UN-independence, everything would go back

to the way it was. At least she wouldn't
have to clean up so much. And get run
over by P.U. dustcarts while chasing runaway buses.

Judy tried to do her homework, but all
the spelling words looked like scrambled
eggs. She tried chewing gum for her ABC
collection, but all it did was stick to her

teeth. She tried starting a scrapbook of her trip to Boston, but even the Declaration of Independence looked sad.

To cheer herself up, Judy wrote a postcard to Tori:

Dear Tori,
Thanks for the tea
(and sugar packets).
They're my fave!
I hAd a tea Party and
got in big trouble! I
chaSed the school bus
(to get my brother)
and got in BIGGER
trouble. I hAve a question.
Cheerios! YNPPFA (Your New Pen Pal from
America),
⊚ * ⊚ * Judy Moody

Victoria MulQueeny
4 Brampton Grove
Harrow, Middlesex
ENGLAND

How do you...
1) stay out of trouble
2) get to do all that
grown-up stuff?
Hurry up and write back!
I'm going barmy!

USA

Judy tiptoed to the top of the stairs to see if she could hear anything. Mum was talking to Stink. Traitor! He was probably blaming the whole thing on her. Redcoat!

Judy climbed back up to her top bunk. "Here, Mouse," called Judy. At least her cat wasn't angry with her. At least her cat was not a traitor.

Mouse hid under the bottom bunk. "Here, Mousie, Mousie." Mouse still did not budge. Even her cat was declaring independence.

Judy's whole room was in a mood. For sure and absolute positive.

After about a hundred years, Stink rattled the doorknob. "Open up!"

"Go away, Stink," Judy told him.

"Open up, honey." That did not sound like Stink. That sounded like Mum. Nice Mum, not Will-You-Ever-Learn Mum.

"We just want to talk to you, Judy." That sounded like Dad. Kind Dad, not You-Are-in-Big-Trouble Dad.

"Am I in big trouble?" Judy asked the door. "Because if I am, then I declare UN-independence. I promise I will NOT make my bed or do my homework or be nice to Stink. And I will definitely NOT rescue him any more. EVER!"

"Judy, open the door so we can talk about this," said Dad.

Judy opened the door. Mum rushed to

hug her. Dad ruffled Judy's hair and kissed the top of her head.

"Stink told us what happened," said Dad. "That was a very brave thing you did."

"It was?"

"I'm sorry, honey," said Mum. "It gave me quite a scare when you two didn't come straight home, so I didn't even stop to listen. You had a hard choice to make and you really used some good, independent thinking."

"I did?"

"You sure did," said Dad.

"I was scared too," said Judy. "I thought a big meany dog might bite me or a

dustcart might run me over or I'd fall and break my head or something. I just kept thinking about Sybil Ludington and how she was scared too."

"We're very proud of you, Sybil," Dad said. "I mean Judy."

"Proud enough to give me more allow-ance and stuff?"

"Dad and I will talk things over," said Mum. "Maybe you *are* ready for a little more independence."

She, Judy Moodington, was not in big-or-little-*T* trouble. And she showed independent thinking. Just like Sybil Ludington.

Star-spangled bananas!

# Yankee Doodle Dandy

After all the excitement, Judy was feeling much too independent to do homework. She got out her Judy Moody Declaration of Independence. This was going straight into her scrapbook.

Judy climbed up to her top bunk. She spread out all the stuff from her trip to Boston. In her scrapbook, she pasted, taped, glue-sticked or Band-Aided all her souvenirs from Boston.

Stink's country pooed on him here

BOSTON CHILDREN'S MUSEUM — ADMIT ONE

BEN FRANKLIN by J.M.

Stink acted like a baby here.

THE PAUL REVERE HOUSE
BOSTON, MASSACHUSETTS

BEAN TOWN

Paul Revere made false teeth and rang bells here (for real!)

Last but not least, she turned the page and glued sugar packets with Ben Franklin sayings onto the page. And she made up a new one:

If at first your brother falls asleep on the bus, ride, ride like Sybil and chase after him.

❂   ❂   ❂

The next day, the story of the not-so-midnight ride of Judy Moody was all over Virginia Dare School.

*Listen, my children, and you shall hear*
*How Judy Moody rode like Sybil and*
*Paul Revere.*

Every time Stink told the story, it got a little wilder. Some heard she was chased by wild wolves. Some heard she was kidnapped by a dustcart. Some heard she fell and broke her leg but kept on riding.

Stink even made Judy a gold medal with a blue ribbon.

❧   ❧   ❧

After dinner that night, Judy climbed up to her top bunk to glue the ribbon into her scrapbook.

The scrapbook was not there! As in G-O-N-E, gone!

She looked under her reading pillow. She looked under lumps of covers and heaps of stuffed animals. She looked under Mouse.

Judy looked all around her room.

The scrapbook was missing. The scrapbook was stolen! By Number One Scrapbook Thief, right here in the Moody house.

"Stink!" Judy ran into his room. "I did not say you could take my scrapbook. Give it!"

"I didn't take your scrapbook," said Stink.

"After I saved your life and everything!" said Judy. "Robber! Stealer! Scrapbook-napper!"

"Am not! I swear on Toady's life I didn't take it."

"If you didn't take it, and I didn't lose it, that leaves Mouse. And Mouse can't read!"

"Maybe Mum and Dad took it," Stink said. "Let's go and ask."

"Let's go and *spy*," said Judy.

Judy and Stink tiptoed down the stairs without too many creaks. They slid across the floor without too many squeaks. They slunk past the living-room, past the kitchen, to Mum's office.

"Stink, you hold the torch. I'll look around." She pawed through the rubbish. She searched on top of the filing cabinet and in the bookshelves.

"Uh-oh!" Stink said. "Check it out!" A message was flashing across Mum's computer screen. It said:

```
JUDY AND STINK,
IF YOU ARE READING THIS,
I KNOW YOU'RE IN HERE.
READ THIS NOTE:
XLOW UVVG ZIV MLG HDVVG.
```

"How can we read it? It's in Russian," Stink said, shining the light on the screen.

"It's not Russian," said Judy. "It's secret code. SPY code. It looks just like Dr Church's secret code in Dad's Freedom Trail book from Boston. Rare!"

"The spy guy? Sweet! We can be code busters, just like him."

"Yep." Judy ran and got her book. She looked it up in the back. "The code is A=Z, B=Y and C=X. All you have to do is use the alphabet backwards."

They looked at the letters again: XLOW UVVG ZIV MLG HDVVG. Judy worked it out. "COLD FEET ARE NOT SWEET. Hmm. It's some sort of clue. Not sweet ... not sweet."

"How about the cookie jar?" Stink asked.

"It says NOT sweet, Stink."

"How about socks? Socks aren't sweet. And they help cold feet."

"Brilliant!" Judy and Stink dashed upstairs, where Judy rummaged through her sock drawer. Sure enough, there was another clue sticking out of her Screamin' Mimi's ice-cream socks.

"It's like a treasure hunt." She opened the note and it read: QFWB GRNVH GDL, YLGS ZIV BLF. She took out her pencil and worked it out in her notebook. "This one says, JUDY TIMES TWO, BOTH ARE YOU."

They thought about it for a long time. They were both stumped. Then Judy got a brainstorm! "There's only one me," said Judy.

"You can say that again," said Stink.

"Unless … I look in a mirror!" Judy and Stink raced for the bathroom. On the bathroom mirror, a message was written in soap crayons: Z SLFHV ULI NLFHV

Stink helped Judy work out the code. "A HOUSE FOR MOUSE!" yelled Judy.

"That doesn't make sense," said Stink.

"Think," said Judy. "What else could be a house for Mouse?"

"Under your bed?" asked Stink. "Or your top bunk?"

"I looked there," said Judy. "Wait! I got it! Where is Mouse whenever we can't find her?"

"The dirty-laundry basket!" said Stink. He ran downstairs after his sister. Judy raced over to the pile of laundry on the washing machine and dug around. "Found it!" she said, holding up her scrapbook.

They flipped through pages of pictures and pebbles, pressed leaves and pencil rubbings, tea bags and sugar packets and Band-Aids, her Declaration of Independence, the postcard from Tori.

She flipped to the last page. She, Judy Moody, was gobsmacked! Glued to the page was a fancy certificate on old-timey paper that looked like parchment.

Hear ye! Hear ye! Judy Moody has hereby . . .

Made her bed every day
Brushed her hair (almost) every day
Done her homework without being asked
Been nice to Stink
Inspired others with her bravery and
courage on her famous ride

. . . which demonstrates independent thinking.
We, the undersigned (Mum and Dad), hereby
grant Judy Moody a 25¢ raise in her allowance,
effective now.
Signed,
Kate Betsy-Ross Moody (aka Mum)
Richard John-Hancock Moody (aka Dad)

Taped to the same page was a shiny new quarter.

"Holy macaroni!" said Judy. "Look! A Maine quarter with a lighthouse! Now I have liberty AND the purse of happiness."

"And with more allowance, you can pay me back a lot faster!" said Stink.

"Wait till I write to Tori and tell her. My Declaration of Independence really worked!"

"Except for the getting your own bathroom thing."

Judy Moody hugged her scrapbook, then Stink. She found Mum and Dad and hugged them too. She even kissed Mouse on her wet pink nose.

"Independence doesn't end here," said Mum. "We're going to expect you to keep being responsible."

"And, of course, you still always have to do your homework," Dad told her.

"And be nice to me!" said Stink.

"Maybe I could also stay up a teeny-weeny bit late? Just for tonight?" asked Judy. "On account of how independent I am now and how I'm not going to be treated like a baby any more and stuff."

"Fifteen minutes," said Dad.

"And just for tonight," said Mum.

Fifteen whole minutes!

"No fair!" said Stink. "Then I'm declaring independence from brushing my teeth! Give me liberty or give me bad breath!"

"One independent kid is enough for now," said Mum. Dad laughed.

֍     ֍     ֍

That night, in those fifteen minutes, Judy ate a snack of grapes and goldfish (the crackers!). She brushed her teeth with red, white and blue toothpaste and washed her face with her very own (Bonjour Bunny) washcloth. She read a whole chapter of her *Ramona the Brave* library book. After only twelve and a half minutes, she couldn't even stay awake any more. She climbed the ladder to her top bunk.

"Lights out!" said Mum. "Goodnight, sweetie." Dad blew her a kiss.

After Mum and Dad pulled the door almost-shut, Judy lay on her top bunk and gazed up at the night-sky ceiling full of glow-in-the-dark stars.

Star-spangled bananas! She, Judy Moody, was Independent-with-a-capital-*I*. As independent as Ben Franklin. John Hancock. Paul Revere. As independent as Sybil Ludington on her midnight ride.

Being independent was brilliant! The bee's knees. And staying up late was Yankee Doodle Dandy.

Judy was getting sleepy. So sleepy. But just before she drifted off, she took out her torch pen and wrote something on the wall, in permanent marker, right next to her pillow:

JUDY MOODY SLEPT HERE.

# The *whole world's* in a Judy Moody mood!

### Say hello to . . .

Fleur Humeur (Judy Moody in the Netherlands)

or Dada Nalada (Judy Moody in Slovakia)

or Hania Humorek (Judy Moody in Poland).

The Judy Moody series has been published in more than twenty countries and languages, for a grand total of more than **12 million books** in print worldwide.

Open up a book – anywhere, any-time – and get ready for your *best mood ever*!

# Have you read them all?

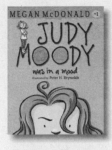

MEGAN McDONALD #1
JUDY MOODY
was in a mood
Illustrated by Peter H. Reynolds

MEGAN McDONALD #2
JUDY MOODY
Gets Famous!
Illustrated by Peter H. Reynolds

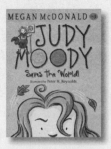

MEGAN McDONALD #3
JUDY MOODY
Saves the World!
Illustrated by Peter H. Reynolds

MEGAN McDONALD #4
JUDY MOODY
Predicts the Future
Illustrated by Peter H. Reynolds

MEGAN McDONALD #5
JUDY MOODY
The Doctor Is In!
Illustrated by Peter H. Reynolds

MEGAN McDONALD #6
JUDY MOODY
Declares Independence!
Illustrated by Peter H. Reynolds

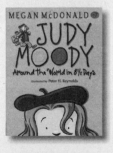

MEGAN McDONALD #7
JUDY MOODY
Around the World in 8½ Days
Illustrated by Peter H. Reynolds

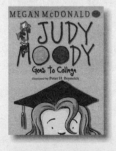

MEGAN McDONALD #8
JUDY MOODY
Goes to College
Illustrated by Peter H. Reynolds

MEGAN McDONALD #9
JUDY MOODY
Girl Detective
Illustrated by Peter H. Reynolds

Judy Moody's
ALL YOU NEED IS A PENCIL!
Double-Rare Way-Not-Boring Book of Fun Stuff to Do
Megan McDonald   Illustrated by Peter H. Reynolds

Judy Moody's
Way Wacky Uber Awesome Book of MORE Fun Stuff to Do
Megan McDonald   Illustrated by Peter H. Reynolds

THE Judy Moody MOOD JOURNAL
Megan McDonald
Illustrated by Peter H. Reynolds

★ ☆ ★ ☆ ★ ☆ ★ ☆ ★ ☆ ★ ☆ ★ ☆ ★ ☆ ★ ☆

# 10 Things You May Not Know About Megan McDonald

10. The first story Megan ever got published (in the fifth grade) was about a pencil sharpener.

9. She read the biography of Virginia Dare so many times at her school library that the librarian had to ask her to give somebody else a chance.

8. She had to be a boring-old pilgrim every year for Halloween because she has four older sisters, who kept passing their pilgrim costumes down to her.

7. Her favourite board game is the Game of Life.

6. She is a member of the Ice-Cream-for-Life Club at Screamin' Mimi's in her hometown of Sebastopol, California.

5. She has a Band-Aid collection to rival Judy Moody's, including bacon-scented Band-Aids.

4. She owns a jawbreaker that is bigger than a baseball, which she will never, ever eat.

3. Like Stink, she had a pet newt that slipped down the drain when she was his age.

2. She often starts a book by scribbling on a napkin.

1. And the number-one thing you may not know about Megan McDonald is: she was once the opening act for the World's Biggest Cupcake!

# 10 Things You May Not Know About Peter H. Reynolds

10. He has a twin brother, Paul. Paul was born first, fourteen minutes before Peter decided to arrive.

9. Peter is part owner of a children's book and toy shop called the Blue Bunny in the Massachusetts town where he lives.

8. He's vertically challenged (aka short!).

7. His mother is from England; his father is from Argentina.

6. He made his first animated film while he was in high school.

5. He sometimes paints with tea instead of water – whatever's handy!

4. He keeps a sketch pad and pen on his nightstand. That way, if an idea hits him in the middle of the night, he can jot it down immediately.

3. His favourite candy is a tie between peanut-butter cups and chocolate-covered raisins (same as Megan McDonald!).

2. One of his favourite books growing up was *The Tall Book of Make-Believe* by Jane Werner, illustrated by Garth Williams.

1. And the number-one thing you may not know about Peter H. Reynolds is: he shares a birthday with James Madison, Stink's favourite president!

# Be sure to check out Stink's adventures too!